P9-DMB-804

Dedicated to all the Marias who
follow the beat of their own drum.

Dedicado a todas las Marías que
siguen su propio ritmo.

—Angela (María Navarrete) Dominguez

Henry Holt and Company, LLC, *Publishers since 1866*
175 Fifth Avenue, New York, New York 10010
mackids.com

Henry Holt® is a registered trademark of Henry Holt and Company, LLC.
Copyright © 2013 by Angela Dominguez
All rights reserved.

Library of Congress Cataloging-in-Publication Data
Dominguez, Angela N.
Maria had a little llama / Angela Dominguez = María tenía una llama pequeña / Angela Dominguez. — 1st ed.
p.   cm.
Summary: In this bilingual version of the classic rhyme, Maria takes her llama to school one day.
ISBN 978-0-8050-9333-9 (hardcover)
[1. Stories in rhyme. 2. Llamas as pets—Fiction. 3. Spanish language materials—Bilingual.]
I. Title. II. Title: María tenía una llama pequeña.
PZ74.3.D7 2013   [E]—dc23   2012013530

First Edition—2013 / Designed by April Ward
Gouache and ink on Arches watercolor board were used to create the illustrations for this book.

Printed in China by South China Printing Co. Ltd., Dongguan City, Guangdong Province

3 5 7 9 10 8 6 4

MARIA HAD A LITTLE LLAMA

MARÍA TENÍA UNA LLAMITA

ANGELA DOMINGUEZ

HENRY HOLT AND COMPANY

NEW YORK

DEC 0 1 2014

PROPERTY OF
SENECA COLLEGE
LIBRARIES
KING CAMPUS

Maria had a little llama

María tenía una llamita

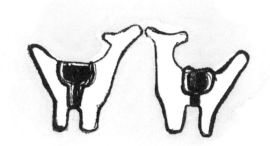

whose fleece was

white as snow.

cuya lana era tan

blanca como la nieve.

And everywhere that Maria went,

Y a donde María iba,

the llama was sure to go.

la llama la seguía.

He followed her to school one day.

Un día la siguió a la escuela.

It made the children laugh and play

to see a llama at school.

Los niños rieron y jugaron

al ver una llama en la escuela.

The teacher had to send him out.

La maestra tuvo que mandarla afuera.

**But still he lingered near
and waited patiently about . . .**

Pero ella se quedó cerca
esperando pacientemente . . .

. . . for Maria to appear!

. . . ¡a que apareciera María!

"Why does the llama love Maria so?"
the eager children cried.
"Maria loves the llama, you know,"
the teacher did reply.

—¿Por qué la llama quiere tanto a María?
—preguntaron ansiosamente los niños.
—Porque María quiere mucho a la llama,
—la maestra respondió.

The End

Fin

PROPERTY OF
SENECA COLLEGE
LIBRARIES
KING CAMPUS